THE LIVER BIRD

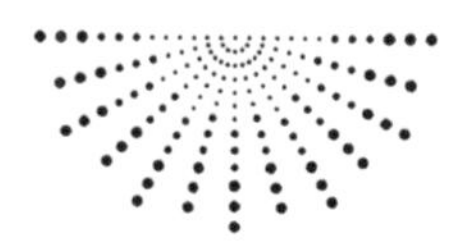

JOHN MAGUIRE

First published in Great Britain in 2019 by
Artgroupie

First published in paperback in 2019

All characters in this book, other than those in the public domain, are fictitious. Any resemblance to real persons, living or dead, is purely coincidental.

A CIP catalogue record for this title is available from the British Library.

ISBN-13: 978-1-9162421-8-0 (paperback edition)
ISBN-13: 978-1-9162421-9-7 (e-book edition)

For Charlie James and all the children of Liverpool

Illustration by Charlie James

MADE IN

THE LIVER BIRD

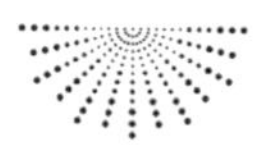

If you did not play football, what did you do? The city was obsessed. Charlie J had tried to play in school and outside with the kids who lived by him in Dauntsey Brow, a bland, grey council estate with an intimidating black warning posted on several walls, 'No Ball Games Allowed!' He possessed a unique ability to hit the ball in completely the opposite way to the direction intended.

After a while, to stop the varied taunts by other kids, he gave up trying to like a sport he despised. Instead, he tended to stay inside the house creating 'episodes' – drama with his Star Wars figures – catastrophic situations like the massacre of the Millennium Falcon. He would crash the spaceship into the stone replica of a pub bar, which was out of place – dominating the tiny living room. It had been built to resemble a Tudor style-drinking den, complete with black and white panelling, wooden beams, empty optics, paper beer mats, and a pineapple ice bucket.

His father, one of the city's many unemployed, would spend weeks constructing a bar, only to become bored quickly, demolish and build it again. It was like Lego on a bigger scale. His father was still a child and had an immaturity that he would never grow out of. Thankfully, Charlie J had inherited his mother's intelligence. His imagination was fertile ground and he would easily lose hours drafting intricate plots and storylines between the plastic figures. With a sharp mind, he already had an ear for picking up dialogue and hook lines.

'He is too bleeding clever for his own good,' his father would often say. It was the only thing he could think to say in response to some of his son's remarks.

Charlie J's bedroom was one of the few spaces in the house that was not covered in woodchip. It was amazing how many rooms were transformed by brightly coloured gloss paint, yet always had woodchip underneath as their foundation. Many times, his mum would roar at him when he was perched at the breakfast bar in the kitchen, absent-mindedly picking at the paper to take out the tiny piece of wood bone underneath. His mum's voice was enough to deter, but on the very rare occasion, it would contain the threat of the slipper: a tartan piece of fabric with an ostentatious gold bow laced through the front, which made it look gift-wrapped, and disguised its sinister objective. The pain the torturous implement could inflict was not as bad as the smell, one that even new inner soles could not extinguish.

. . .

Grandma Bailey and Charlie J would go on a bus ride every Sunday to the Pier Head. This meant sweets, doughnuts, and a visit to the chippy. The steaming hot potatoes would mould themselves to the white paper. Tucking your hand in would give a short respite from the cold, but then the heat from the sweaty salted spuds could be just as harsh, if not harsher.

The day would routinely begin with a trip to St Paschal Baylon for the early church service, all incense, chanting and ringing bells, to disguise the intense loneliness of the parishioners and the priest. There was safety in dwindling numbers. The Catholic mass was Charlie J's first exposure to theatricality, planting the seeds of a later acting career.

When Grandma Bailey held his hand, her skin was spider-web thin, and so soft to the touch, he could feel the delicate bones. She smelt of a nondescript perfume and Glacier Mints. She had an endless supply in her handbag. Inside the leather bag, you could see a batch of faded envelopes, containing letters she carried everywhere after she lost her husband William. The correspondence that they had engaged in during their courtship before his premature death in his early twenties. The letters were worn at the edges and had been opened, read, and refolded often.

The first time Charlie J really saw inside the bag was when she had to retrieve a tissue from deep in its cellar. A seagull dropped an offering on Charlie J as they walked through the city centre past the many boarded-up shop windows. It streaked through his blond hair and made a detailed pathway along his red jacket.

'It's good luck, son,' muttered Grandma Bailey. Charlie J failed to comprehend the logic behind this belief; the same thinking behind the rabbit foot attached to her keys. That too was meant to bring good luck, but it was not exactly lucky for the rabbit, thought the inquisitive child.

They would ride into town on the top deck of what Charlie J's mum referred to as 'the tramp chariot'. As the number 79 propelled them up the Childwall Valley Hill, the tree branches tried to pull the bus back down, crashing and slapping at the windows. Grandma Bailey loved the greenery of Belle Vale, a contrast from the Dingle and the drab claustrophobic tenement she had been brought up in. Her favourite time of the year was autumn when the yellow, orange, and brown leaves took over from the summer's pink wedding confetti scattered over the bus.

The walk from the bus stop to the Pier Head could be brutal, depending on the mood of Madame Le Mersey. She would sometimes peck a few salty kisses on the cheek but other times it would be a full-on ravishing.

'It's facelift wind,' Charlie J declared.

'What, love?' questioned Grandma Bailey.

'Facelift wind! Mum says that when the wind is so strong it can blow away the years.'

'Oh, my goodness, there's a thought!' She laughed. 'I don't know about wind, love, I would need a hurricane to fix this face!'

Her appearance was lined, and Charlie J wondered if each line represented a year, like trees. If that was the case, his grandma must be ancient, nearly as old as the Allerton Oak in Calderstones Park. When his father was employed for a relatively short time as a gravedigger in Springwood cemetery, he would take Charlie to the football field in Calderstones, sometimes three times a week. Now that he had more time on his hands, owing to being unemployed, he never took his boy out anymore.

The Allerton Oak

The Pier Head terminal was a shed, a two-storey monstrosity, pebble-dashed in seagull droppings. Charlie J and Grandma Bailey would orientate to one of the better seats on the top promenade's viewing platform, drifting through the chewed-up mouldy wooden benches to find one to look out to sea and over to the flatness of

Birkenhead. Bombs had desecrated that side of the river during the war, when residents had allegedly been encouraged to keep the lights on in the May Blitz of 1941 to trick the enemy into thinking it was the Liverpool docks.

The stench from the doughnut store below rose through the decking. A sugary substance that choked if you caught it on an in-breath. There was also a chip shop that was like a heroin-addicted version of a normal chip shop, and a traditional sweet shop. These stores would not be allowed to operate in today's hygiene-rated safe society. Back then, nobody cared. Nobody cared about anything in the stagnant Pool of Life. A prosperous city had been left to fend for itself, dressed in a thin decaying cloak called 'managed decline.'

You could look at the Mersey every single day and she never looked the same. The waters could bring calmness in the mind. Sometimes it was so algid that to sit there could not be endured for more than five minutes. Generally, the two would look out on the top, taking in the sea air for a good fifteen minutes before the old lady would pipe up. 'Come on then, best be off.'

Each week before they headed up Water Street to catch the bus, Grandma Bailey would always pause and greet the two statues perched on the top of the Liver Building. 'Good morning, Mrs Liver Bird. Good morning, Mr Liver Bird.'

'What is a Liver Bird?' Charlie asked her once.

His grandma, who was usually economic with her

words – unless she was regaling historical facts – gave him the full story,

'See those two, Charlie J? The female Liver Bird is looking out over the River Mersey, protecting all those who are working the waters, checking they're safe. The male Liver Bird is guarding the city to shield its inhabitants. Also, to see what time the pubs open. If the pair turn around and look at each other, they will fall hopelessly in love and fly away together, to build a new nest. Liverpool will crumble into the sea.'

'What nonsense!' Charlie J replied.

'Yes, true, but do you know something, lad? When the two came down to be cleaned back in the 1950s, the council kept them in a warehouse in exactly the same position, so as not to evoke the superstition. Just imagine, Charlie J, being a sailor and looking through the telescope and catching sight of those pair on the horizon, you would know you were home.'

'Are they real birds?'

'Oh no, pure fiction. King John, who created Liverpool, had a wax seal, like a stamp, and the symbol on it was an eagle. Nobody had ever seen an eagle, but they had seen a duck and a cormorant. Like a lot of the people in the city, the Liver Bird was made by accident.'

'Why then are there different birds around town? Some look fierce, others are like muppets.'

'There are many different interpretations, lad, but they're all meant to be the same.'

'Like Batman?'

'Yes, like Batman, I suppose, sweetheart. That's one way of looking at it.'

'What is in its mouth?'

'In the birds' beaks, there is generally a piece of seaweed to remind us that Liverpool is only wealthy because of the waters.'

'Is it a vegetarian like Mum's friend Gwyn?'

Grandma laughed loudly. 'Oh yes, I'd never thought of it like that.'

One Sunday in February, the Mersey in its murky stillness looked as blank as Grandma Bailey. The waters had an undercurrent of emerald green, occasionally shimmering through like a starling's feathers.

They sat casting their eyes out to sea. Charlie J always believed that as he perched there, the bench transformed into a sturdy throne and he surveyed the river as if it were his own. He was King John and the bus shelter was the Castle of Liverpool. He was overseeing the construction of the fishing village, turning the muddy pool into a thriving port, or watching his troops going off to Ireland.

The seagulls screeched and sang out, like a Liverpool mother calling her kids in from the street. A contagion of the birds surveyed the land for food, some from the sky, others foot soldiers, tottering around the pavements on a covert mission to seek out sustenance. At times, their squawking was like a coded language.

In the distance, over Cammell Laird, Charlie J noticed one bird standing out from the other gulls as it gracefully weaved through the air. He pointed at the creature.

'Look, Grandma, look at that one! It's a Liver...'

She pretended to look at the bird. 'Oh, they are lovely, aren't they, my dear?' she uttered on autopilot. Her eyes glazed over, he could tell she was physically there, but her mind was elsewhere.

The bird's plumage glistened in the light: metallic silver with an undercoating of amethyst. It looked like it had flown straight off the pages of the *Audubon Book of Birds*, encased in the Oak Room in Central Library. He caught sight of a golden yellow beak and razor-sharp, webbed claws, like pointed HB pencils, as it darted past, camouflaged amongst the other birds. It craned its head to look directly at Charlie J. He looked it in the eye and was transported to another world. It did not just see him, it made a connection. A warm, glowing feeling of pure joy flooded through the little boy.

'It has chosen to appear to me, just me. JUST ME!' he thought to himself. As soon as the thought occurred to him, the bird puffed up its plumage and bolted away.

That night Charlie J lay tucked up in bed with the staircase light on and the door open a fraction. His mind raced with the image of the bird. It became even more beautiful the more he thought about it. The creature moved with such grace and appeared aware of how elegant it looked. Charlie J wished he could have a small portion of that confidence. That would stop Jimmy Lamb from pinching his arm and being nasty to him.

He could not sleep, so he decided to get his book from its hiding place and read. Charlie J's favourite book was one that detailed vocabulary. It consisted of many different places, 'At the beach,' 'At the garage,' and then all the words that you would associate with that location were listed. He chose 'At the dock,' and scanned through the list repeatedly but there was no listing for Liver Bird at all. If it is not in a book does it not exist?

He cupped his hands and made the shape of a bird's beak against the spotlight beam of his torch. A Liver Bird was projected onto his stars-and-space wallpaper. For a fleeting few seconds, the actual profile of the bird appeared in its silver elegance and then faded away. The groaning creak of the lower staircase signalled one of his parents was ascending, so he snapped off the torch, put his book under the pillow and feigned deep sleep. He had stopped employing the heavy breathing technique as his overtly dramatic performance made it obvious that he was faking it. He was well practised in this cover-up routine and soon flying into the realms of sleep, immersed in a dreamscape of gigantic multi-coloured bird feathers.

Charlie J had to stay behind before the morning break as the teacher wanted to congratulate him on his reading. He walked onto the schoolyard very pleased with himself. Jimmy Lamb stood away from the gang with a sly smile emblazoned on his face. The four other boys began whispering to each other, cupping their hands over the other's ear, and then looking at Charlie J. They would whisper a phrase or mutter under their breath.

'What did you say?' Charlie J uttered nervously. The

troupe repeated his line in unison and continued to chant it at him over and over.

Jimmy Lamb looked on, surveying his handiwork; this was one of his head-working pranks.

Realising this was going to be the game for the rest of the break, Charlie J turned around and headed back indoors to take sanctuary in the library. To be honest, he preferred twenty minutes' adventure in a storybook than to feel so alone on the yard. Even amongst this gaggle of fair-weather friends, he felt on the outside. Books took you places, and when immersed in a story, you were never ever truly on your own.

From then on Charlie J kept his eyes focused on the rooftops and skies of Liverpool. There was no sign of anything otherworldly at all. Once he thought he saw the Liver Bird on top of the art gallery, sitting next to the statue of Lady Liverpool, but it was only an angry gull screeching abuse, a feathered form of Tourette's syndrome. On a wet, sloppy, cross-country run in Court Hey Park during his PE lesson, he was excited at a figure in a tree and ran towards it, to discover it was only a bin bag entangled.

The Liver Bird

Every Sunday for the next few weeks, he was desperate to get through the church service and make it to the Pier Head. The bus journey seemed to take forever. Grandma Bailey was amused that he no longer pleaded for the sugary wrongness of doughnuts on arrival at their destination, but instead simply wanted to sit and look out to sea.

One day she had said chuckling, 'That old girl the Mersey has really got you under her spell, hasn't she?'

Each week he looked on with bated breath. Each week, there was no reappearance of the Liver Bird. The winter weather started to become so unpredictable that they no longer knew if they were going on a bus trip on a Sunday until the actual morning. In school, Jimmy Lamb became unpredictable too. Sometimes he would let Charlie J join in and play games with him, other times he would turn nasty. Particularly when the rest of the gang laughed and included him. If kept on the periphery it was okay, but the moment he took a little of the spotlight then Jimmy Lamb's mood transformed.

In assembly one morning, Jimmy sat next to Charlie J cross-legged. The assembly hall floor always smelt of polish. The school had its own odour: a mix of bleach, cleaning products and stewed cabbage from the canteen. Charlie J was focused on the teacher who was retelling another story about Jesus. He could not understand how Jesus was born in the Middle East yet had white skin. Perhaps another one of the many miracles he performed. Charlie J decided it best not to ask the teachers that question. He understood some things should not be questioned; it was easier that way.

The boys in the school all had shorts on even though it was wintry weather conditions. Up close, you could really see how bad Jimmy Lamb's eczema was. Charlie J had seen Jimmy Lamb's mother goading him one night when she picked him up from school, calling him a 'midget leper'. It was good of Jimmy Lamb's mum to pick him up from school when she was clearly sick, thought Charlie J. She always drove to collect him in her pyjamas.

As they sat in the assembly, which seemed to go on forever, Jimmy Lamb picked off a scab and placed the dead skin in his mouth. He did this as if it was the most natural thing to do. He caught Charlie J looking and his shocked gaze reminded him he was in school and not at home alone. The embarrassment blotted over his face like a stain. He looked like he was about to cry before a hatred flooded over. Jimmy Lamb was notably horrible to Charlie J after that event.

'The Bluecoat was called the Bluecoat because when the school opened, the poor children who attended wore blue coats.' Grandma Bailey and Charlie J had jumped off the bus early as the rain pelted the tramp chariot with sharp wet spears, so instead of going to the Pier Head, she had taken Charlie J for a meander around the gallery and for some food.

'I won't be able to enter then, Grandma.'

'Why ever not, love?'

'My coat is red!' he chuckled.

'Oh, Charlie J, you are a one. Did you know this is the oldest building in the city centre?'

The two trotted into the Queen Anne-style entrance through the courtyard. They ordered the Scouse and sat down to eat.

'Scouse is the dish of Liverpool, the Scandinavian sailors brought the recipe here, it's mutton, potatoes, and carrots. Oh, and gravy.'

'What is mutton?'

'Most of the girls on Mathew Street on a Saturday night.'

'What, Nan?'

'Sorry, love, I am just being facetious. Mutton is old lamb. During the war, we had no choice but to have blind Scouse as meat supplies were so low and rationed.'

'The Liver Bird would eat blind Scouse, Nan.'

'What do you mean, love?'

'Well, it's vegetarian, isn't it? Seaweed in its mouth like on the gates there.' Charlie J pointed to the sturdy black iron gates that had the emblem sculpted on the top.

'Well spotted, love, and there's one above the entrance door. Two of the oldest birds in town, even older than me,' she declared. 'You know, love, I did tell you the Liver Bird is everywhere in this city, you just have to look for it – really look for it.'

Grandma Bailey looked Charlie J in the eye and, for an instant, he thought he saw the very Mersey waters wave through her pupils. She seemed to hint to him about his Liver Bird. Did Grandma Bailey know? Perhaps she was a white witch. She did have a cat and ground up herbs in a pestle and mortar. Perhaps that was her cauldron that had been shrunk by a rival witch. And, of course, she refused to have a vacuum cleaner, instead opting for an old-fashioned broomstick.

Charlie J kept his eye on the doorway. Grandma Bailey was talking about the overhead electric railway, another history lesson, the same story Charlie J had heard repeatedly. Outside a winged creature fluttered past and circled in the air as if looking for something. The

Liver Bird hovered and dropped onto the gate sitting next to the metal replica.

Charlie J rose rapidly and scrambled to the door. He bumped into the waitress who was balancing three cheese toasties up her arm. The server managed to hold on to the plates but the impact of the little bowling ball of a kid sent her spinning. Charlie J had completely zoned out and his ears were immune to the shouting reproachment of his grandma.

The Liver Bird looked a little forlorn, its plumage haggard, and before Charlie J could get out of the door, it flew off. There was only the scary clown at the gates; the man, who sold deformed balloons, looked like he had blown the family fortune, amassed from generations of a traditional circus, and become ravaged by drugs. The dirty-faced joker stared at Charlie J and gave a slow calculated wave, hoping he would pester his parent to buy an overpriced bag of air.

Grandma Bailey yanked him back inside and he said sorry to the waitress as instructed, but he was not present, his mind was with his Liver Bird.

The two sat by the river in their usual spot. Grandma Bailey looked over to the staircase and saw a young mum struggling to carry a pram upstairs; she had two other kids in tow. 'Mummy, I want to go up to the viewing platform. I want to see the ships, please, Mummy.'

'Freddie, I can't get up the stairs with the baby.'

'But please, Mummy.'

Something about her plight was all too familiar to Grandma Bailey; she vaulted from her seat.

'Hang on, love, let me help you.' She sped over to assist the mum with her climb.

Charlie J scanned his eyes across the river. Today the clear water was completely flat with an occasional twitch rippling across and then a return to stillness. The river was like a giant mirror, reflecting the light lapis lazuli heavens. What looked like a giant exclamation mark hung in the sky. He thought it was probably a seagull hovering but, as it flapped towards the shore, Charlie J recognised it.

The bird flew with a grace and dexterity that stood out and drew your eye. It was flying directly to him. It landed on the splintered concourse with precision, an arm's distance away. The bird surveyed the environment. Charlie J was all alone, just him and the bird. He felt honoured that he had chosen to wait and give him a private audience. The bird looked through him, before suddenly spotting a discarded bag of chips on a decrepit bench. It flitted over and swiftly started to work on the contents.

The Liver Bird was not here to see Charlie J at all; it did not even care. It wanted to feed its face on filthy greasy rubbish. Charlie J stared, hoping for some sort of recognition or a sign to indicate he was wrong in his judgements of the bird's actions. That tatty bird just carried on greedily gobbling the leftover food. It was not bothered if it ate part of the paper either! A feral rough thing, it was. Up close, its feathers looked dirty too.

Grandma was now busy chatting away with the young mother at the top of the stairs. Her other children, free from the pram, were running around hyperactive and bored in the far corner of the viewing platform. The mood soured and a stinking waft seeped from the Mersey. Grandma was cornered in her conversation; the mum obviously did not talk to many people in the course of her day. Grandma gave an occasional glance over at Charlie J to check all was okay, the natural maternal streak.

The Liver Bird continued unabashed, guzzling away. A wave of anger boiled through Charlie J's body. How dare this winged fiend fly here and totally ignore him. He had waited for weeks to spot the Liver Bird and now it had appeared and shown him no respect. It did not care.

Charlie J noticed the empty banana milkshake carton next to him on the bench. Grandma Bailey had instructed him to keep it until they found a suitable bin, one that was not overflowing. An empty bin was as rare in the city as a real live Liver Bird. He picked it up and launched the plastic missile directly at the creature. It made a rattle as it sped and bounced around the tarmac. It had missed but stopped the beast consuming its meal.

The bird looked Charlie J directly in the eye. Was there a sign of sadness? Within seconds, it raised its mighty wings, blocking out the light. It looked like a Pegasus. The bird was transformed to be even more dazzling than he had first seen. It stood on its legs, prehistoric in its beauty, flapped its wings once and flew off into an approaching cloud. The sky was awash with cotton-wool clouds, like dried-up mashed potato. In a moment, the bird was out of sight. What had he done? His winged friend was disappointed, Charlie J knew it. Would he ever see it again? Or had he blown his chance completely? He felt shame and utter disgust.

'Hey, lad, your face looks as moody as the sky! Cheer up, it might never happen.'

Grandma Bailey was ready to head home before the heavens wept.

'Come on, son, let's get you back.'

Charlie J was quiet the entire journey home.

He heard his grandma mumbling something to his mum. 'He must be coming down with something because he's been silent most of the day.'

His mum knew that was not at all like him. Charlie J was famed in the family for his inquisitive nature and the ability to talk non-stop. In some cases, he could even talk in his sleep. He decided to play along with Grandma Bailey's diagnosis and asked if he could go and lie down in his room.

Charlie J looked at the ceiling and wondered why people ever thought that Artex looked good. It turned into smeared cake dough, layered like seagull crap as it aged.

Before he could follow that train of thought, Charlie J heard a deafening screech and jumped up to look out his window; the Canadian geese were back for the winter and sang their airborne karaoke as they flew towards Hale village. There was no sign of his Liver Bird; he had blown it, completely blown it. Charlie J threw his head down on his pillow in frustration and sickness started to develop in his stomach. Perhaps he had thought himself sick.

The next day Charlie J had been in the library for most of the lunch hour. He loved the smell of the books and a wall of books next to his chair gave him a great feeling of comfort, as well as making him feel safe. An encyclopaedia of birds was his latest obsession; he had pored over it for the last few weeks. He had hoped that it might telepathically signal something to the Liver Bird: to acknowledge he was not one of those children who were cruel to birds and that he was extremely sorry for his actions.

'You can take that book home with you for the weekend, if you promise to take really good care of it.' Mrs Lightbody, the librarian had interrupted his pondering. She had noticed how attached the boy had become to this particular book.

'Can I, miss? That would be fantastic. Thank you.'

'You have impeccable manners, young man, it's my pleasure. I wish more of your class would read like you. Readers are leaders, remember that.'

'Yes, miss, thank you.'

There was still five minutes of playtime left, so Charlie J decided to leave this space as the librarian's attention was becoming a little bit embarrassing. He could sense an approaching lecture.

'Have a nice weekend and thanks again,' he chirped.

He sat on the far side of the playground by the trees, away from everybody. Jimmy Lamb and his gang of five were taunting the girls with a football. He immersed himself in the book. He was reading about the robin as dark shadows cast over the open pages. Jimmy Lamb and his mates surrounded him in a circle.

'Look at the little bookworm,' squeaked Jimmy Lamb. His gang repeated the phrase in unison. Charlie J sprang up, so he was no longer at a disadvantage. Jimmy Lamb pushed him and shouted in his face, 'Reading is for sissies, bookworm.'

'Bookworm, bookworm, bookworm,' the group sang out, repeating the taunt in the type of high-pitched noise that would cause a dog distress.

'How would you know, Lamb head? You can't read.'

'What did you say?'

'Please leave me alone. I want to read my book, please.'

'No, repeat what you said, Nancy boy.'

'Leave me alone.'

Charlie J tried to avoid eye contact with Jimmy Lamb. Clearly, this was not something of which Jimmy wanted to let go. He pushed Charlie J, jolting the book out of his hands and onto the muddy grass. It landed face down, smearing the open page, now showing a grass-stained cormorant. The rest of his crew stopped chanting as their game was taking a different turn. Charlie J looked at the smug smile planted on Jimmy Lamb's face and all the thoughts of never seeing the Liver Bird again flooded through his tiny body. He shoved Jimmy Lamb, sending him sprawling to the ground

The bully was shocked at this unpredicted uprising. Charlie J stood waiting for Jimmy to pounce back. His face charged with a knowing confidence that radiated an unsettling strength. For the first time, Jimmy was not sure how to respond. He sat for what seemed like an entirety but was really a few seconds. This action sent an unspoken signal to the rest of his gang of followers. But before this weakness could be further exploited, the tobacco-scented hairy arms of the break supervisor dragged Jimmy up off the ground and barked orders for the two to get inside to speak to the head teacher.

That night Charlie could hear tapping on the window of his bedroom. In his half-asleep state, he figured it must be the long, withered branch of the silver birch. The tree scratched its claw lightly in the breeze and more violently in stormy weather.

The noise was consistent and eventually he sprang out of bed to look. As he did, he noticed the dark silhouette of the Liver Bird. He froze. Was he dreaming? The bird was even more bedazzling than before and now its feathers appeared technicolour, with colours Charlie J had never seen before. It opened up its golden yellow beak and gave an angelic cry, looking at him as it had on their first encounter.

Charlie edged closer to the window, slowly so as not

to startle the bird. He was illuminated by the entrancing glow radiating off the creature.

The bird was not at all perturbed and stayed for a moment as the boy's face touched the cold glass pane and then vanished. Charlie stared out into the garden. The silver birch waltzed slowly in the night breeze and, in the distance, he could see the light-blur of cars on the motorway. The moon hung like a pale milk lantern. There was no trace of the bird. Charlie wondered again whether he had been dreaming. Perhaps, he decided. He opened the window to let the cool breeze whistle into the room.

Then he noticed it. On the window ledge, a huge feather glistened. It was the colour of amethyst. Charlie carefully manoeuvred the feather into the room, taking heed of his mum's warnings about opening the window. The feather lit up the dark space. It was still warm. He placed it carefully on the table as he lunged to find the treasure chest he kept under his bed. He desperately tried to do this without making a sound. Whenever you do not want to make a noise purposefully, that is when you are most likely to make a noise.

He tenderly placed the feather in a cardboard box and put it in the wooden trunk that Grandma Bailey had given him. It was one of the few possessions that had been his grandfather's. He stuck a note on the cardboard lid warning to KEEP OUT. DO NOT DISTURB. PRIVATE.

ABOUT THE AUTHOR

AUTHOR BIOGRAPHY

John Maguire is a playwright and leads history walking tours around his home town of Liverpool. His play chronicling the life of Catherine Wilkinson, the founder of the first public washhouse in the UK after the cholera epidemic, *Kitty: Queen of the Washhouse* and this fable, *The Liver Bird*, were both inspired from his weekly walking tours. John also writes for the magazine *Ten Million Hardbacks*, 10mh.net

ILLUSTRATOR BIOGRAPHY

Suzi Dorey is an illustrator, a scenographer and runs her own creative business, Suzi Dorey Design https://www.suzidoreydesign.com

MADE IN

Lightning Source UK Ltd.
Milton Keynes UK
UKHW011230040922
408286UK00002B/55